CW01374025

Gina Bains

The Angel and Her Companion

Austin Macauley Publishers™
LONDON • CAMBRIDGE • NEW YORK • SHARJAH

Copyright © Gina Bains (2017)

The right of Gina Bains to be identified as author of this work has been asserted by her in accordance with section 77 and 78 of the Copyright, Designs and Patents Act 1988.

All rights reserved. No part of this publication may be reproduced, stored in a retrieval system, or transmitted in any form or by any means, electronic, mechanical, photocopying, recording, or otherwise, without the prior permission of the publishers.

Any person who commits any unauthorised act in relation to this publication may be liable to criminal prosecution and civil claims for damages.

A CIP catalogue record for this title is available from the British Library.

ISBN 9781787108080 (Paperback)
ISBN 9781787108097 (E-Book)
www.austinmacauley.com

First Published (2017)
Austin Macauley Publishers Ltd.
25 Canada Square
Canary Wharf
London
E14 5LQ

Chapter One

"My child, I must go now but will always watch over you and always be there for you."

When the light went out, Angel opened her eyes. Her Companion guided her towards the bed and moved the pillow so that Angel could see the gift that the Lord had left for her. It was a gold chain with a white pearl on.

Straight away Angel put her necklace on and looked into the mirror; she knew it was the necklace that had the powers in.

Angel looked at Companion and said, "Do you know how to use this lovely necklace for powers?"

Companion nodded his head and said, "Yes," then Angel knelt down, prayed to the Lord and said, "Thank you so much for choosing me to help people in need. I will never let anyone know the truth about myself; I will never disappoint you, my Lord."

After Angel finished her prayers, there was a knock on her door; it was her brother, who said, "I left your food outside your door."

Angel replied, "Please take the food away as I am not hungry," so her brother took the food away but nobody came back to ask Angel why she was not hungry or why she refused to eat. Nobody had any interest in asking Angel those questions, as the family were too busy in their own lives.

Angel sat on her bed with Companion in her arms, wearing her dress and the mask, and said to Companion, "After midnight, can we go out for a while? It's been a long time since I have been out and had any fresh air. I feel suffocated in this room."

Companion nodded his head and said, "Yes" and when it was midnight and everyone was asleep, Companion went towards the window and Angel said, "If I go through the window, I may fall out and hurt myself."

Companion moved away from the window and started to fly around the room towards the window, then gave Angel signs that she could also fly.

Angel understood the signs and she began to fly around her room and, with a big smile on her face, through the window with Companion.

Angel could not believe she could fly. She looked at Companion and said, "This is the happiest day of my life. I can go anywhere I wish, and we will always fly together."

Companion was on Angel's shoulder as they flew away and she saw all the beauty she had missed whilst she was sick.

Angel noticed there was a little dog whose leg was trapped between two metal bars so she and Companion went down to help the creature.

Angel looked at Companion and said, "How do I help this dog who is in so much pain?"

Companion touched the white pearl on Angel's necklace three times, then Angel had the powers and put her hands on the dog to heal the wounds on his leg and set him free.

Angel said to Companion, "It's time to go back home now before anyone finds out that I am not there," so they flew back home through the window and Angel, feeling so happy said to Companion, "This all feels like a dream, I am so happy and lucky. I can go out and help people and animals."

While Angel got changed, she said to Companion, "Where can I hide my dress, the mask and the gloves where no one will find them?"

Companion went behind the wardrobe and Angel followed the bird as it wound its way to the secret small room which no one knew about. As Companion and Angel went into this secret room, there was a lot of old small items.

Angel looked at Companion and said, "This will be the safest place to keep the dress and the mask," which she then put in the old trunk.

Then she gave the necklace that had powers to Companion and said, "You find a safe place for this."

Companion found the perfect place, which was behind an old picture that was on the wall. After that, they locked the door to the secret room and came out and Angel and Companion lay on the bed.

Angel was thinking of all the amazing things that had taken place all day and, looking at Companion, said, "This is the beginning of a new journey of my life. And so many changes will take place, all in good time. I am so honoured and blessed to have been chosen to bring changes into people's lives and show them the important things that matter in life."

As Angel was talking to Companion, she fell asleep.

Chapter Two

Early the next morning there was a knock on her bedroom door which was her brother who left breakfast for her outside her door.

As Angel opened the door, she said, "Good morning" to her older brother, John with a big smile on her face. He was really surprised to see his sister so happy for the first time since she had had the incident.

John said, "Why are you so happy, Angel?"

She replied, "Everything will get better soon."

John was confused by the reply he had got from his litter sister Angel and went downstairs to tell his mother in the kitchen.

"I don't think Angel is OK. I'm worried about her and it's not fair that she should be locked in her bedroom, day and night."

The mother, whose name was Anna said to her son, "John, don't worry about your sister, Angel, as I know what's best for her.

"I am her mother," she continued. "You're getting late for school, your brother James and your father are waiting for you outside. Have a good day at school."

John left for school thinking, on his way, that the way his sister Angel was being treated wasn't fair.

He told his father, whose name was Adam and his brother James, and his father replied, "My son, there is not much I can do. I have left everything in God's hands as he knows what's best for Angel and I've also left it in your mother's hands as she knows what's best for Angel and the family.

"You can never tell anyone that you and John have a sister named Angel. If people find out that you boys have a sister who has diseases, we will all get thrown out of our home and it will break your mother's heart. I don't have the energy or the strength to rebuild and start again, so you boys will have to promise me you will never mention Angel to anyone or even bring the subject up again."

Meanwhile, back at home Angel's mother Anna went to Angel's bedroom to collect the breakfast dishes and said to Angel, "Why are you so happy and acting differently?"

Angel replied, "Mother, nothing is wrong. I am fine and I am not angry any more. I am not upset just because you lock me in my bedroom day and night to the extent that I am not allowed to go outside to play.

"It's OK, Mother. You know what's best for me because you're my mother."

Angel's mother was surprised with Angel's behaviour.

Angel asked her mother if she could bring her drawing papers and tins of paint, as she loved painting and it was some time since she had done any.

Angel's mother got what Angel had asked for and also told her daughter that she was happy that she finally accepted her fate of never leaving her bedroom or ever going outside.

"The only day you will go is when the Lord takes you. Until then you can do whatever you like in your bedroom.

That's where you remain until your last days, but remember not to make any noises or stand by the window. If anyone sees you, then you will be in big trouble."

Angel promised her mother that she would not have any problem with her and no one would ever find out about her. Angel looked up into her mother's eyes and said, "I am not afraid of dying if that's what the Lord wants. If that is the case, who am I to question the Lord and who said I am alone? I've got the Lord with me; his angels are watching me. And I also have you, my mother, my father and my brothers. I am very lucky to be loved and very happy my name is Angel and the most important thing is, I have my faith that keeps me strong and am blessed because I was born on the same day as Jesus: 25th December."

Angel's mother Anna was so speechless she ended up giving Angel a hug, cried and said, "Forgive me my child."

Angel replied, "You have nothing to feel sorry for, or to ask forgiveness for, for we are all being tested by God."

Angel's mother Anna was shocked, walked out of Angel's bedroom feeling guilty, locked her bedroom door and went downstairs asking herself where her child got all these wise words from.

"I see something different in my child Angel. Maybe it's my mind playing games with me." And Angel's mother Anna continued with her daily routine and house chores as Angel was painting with Companion in the secret room which was behind the wardrobe, before her mother entered into the bedroom.

Angel told Companion, "My mother has changed since the incident took place. I believe my mother Anna has lost her faith in God. But one day her faith will come back, but until then there is a lot we both need to see in the outside world. So after midnight we will go out and will fly in the neighbourhood and will see what is going on. We'll enjoy the adventure as I never got to see my neighbours, the shops, and the school where my brothers John and James study. The only place I saw when I came to this city was the church. I was sitting outside the church with my family covered in the blanket as if I didn't exist. We were all homeless."

Companion just looked at Angel and smiled while she was talking. There was a knock on the bedroom door and Angel was shocked.

She said to Companion, "It's not supper time yet so who can that be?"

So Angel left Companion in the secret room went into her bedroom to open the door and it was her brother John. Angel opened the door and said, "What are you doing?"

"I had to see you, Angel. Can I please come in before anyone sees me outside your room?" So Angel let her brother inside her bedroom and John said, "You are my little sister, Angel and I miss playing with you and I hate the fact you are always locked in your bedroom and not allowed outside. I am your big brother and I will always be there for you."

Angel replied, "If our parents find out, you will get into trouble. John, it's best you leave."

John said, "I'll only leave if you promise me, Angel we can sometimes spend time together when everyone is asleep."

Angel agreed and John gave Angel a hug and some sweets before he left. Angel was so happy that her brother cared about her. This meant a lot to Angel, and she said to Companion, "We need to be more careful now because my brother John will be coming to my bedroom. Soon it will be dark then we'll go out."

John came to Angel's room later to give her supper and told her, "I will see you tomorrow."

Angel replied, "I will be looking forward to seeing you, my brother John."

Angel locked her bedroom door, had her supper and got ready to go out. As soon as it was dark, Angel said to Companion, "I was looking forward to this all day when it's going to be dark, so I can wear my Angel outfit so we can go out and see the beauty."

As Angel and Companion were flying, they went across one house where a little boy was playing in his bedroom with his ball. Angel said to Companion, "How come he is still awake and not asleep? Please go and find out."

So Companion went to the little boy's bedroom window as it was open, and Companion was making noises and the little boy looked around and could hear the bird.

The boy said, "I can't see. Are you OK?"

Companion knew the boy was blind but he could hear. Angel was on the other side where she could see the boy but he couldn't see her, so Angel and Companion went into the little boy's bedroom.

Angel said, "Please don't be afraid. I am your friend," but the little boy was afraid and said, "Who are you?"

Angel replied, "I am your friend and this bird's name is Companion. Would you like to hold him?"

The boy said yes and Angel said, "What is your name?"

The boy said, "My name is Abrielle," and Angel said, "It's a nice name."

"And how come you're not asleep yet, Abrielle?"

He replied, "I am not happy because I can't see and children at my school bully me because I am blind and poor. I have loving parents including my dog Buzzo, but I have no friends and I'll never be able to see again; I will always be blind."

Angel replied, "My dear friend Abrielle, your life will change and you already have a friend which is me, Angel and from today onwards only good things will happen in your life, that's a promise."

Abrielle was so happy and said, "Is this a dream?"

Angel replied, "No, Abrielle, it's true. Now you go to sleep, and I will see you tomorrow night."

Abrielle smiled and went to sleep. Companion and Angel flew through Abrielle's bedroom window.

As Angel and Companion were traveling in the village, they came across many people who were unhappy, fighting with each other and struggling.

They came across a big house which resembled a palace and saw a little girl called Mary standing by the window in her bedroom looking at the stars and saying, "I don't want to die; I want to get better. Please answer my prayers, my Lord."

As Mary walked away from her bedroom window and went towards her bed, Companion and Angel came through the window. And when Mary looked back, she was so speechless and shocked to see Companion and Angel.

She froze but blurted out, "Who are you, what are you doing in my bedroom?"

Angel replied, "Your prayers will be answered soon, Mary. You must be patient, it's a test from God to see how strong your faith is. One day, we all must go to the Lord and no one can live forever."

Angel asked Mary, "So, tell me everything about yourself, before and after you got ill, and how it happened."

Mary was sitting on the bed and she begun to tell Angel everything from the beginning. "I lived here in this village called Grace Village. From the moment I was born I had a happy childhood, with loving parents but no brothers or sisters, but I have many friends who care about me. My parents love me so much they buy me anything I want, as you can see in my bedroom. I have every toy and pretty dresses, I have everything that a child can wish for. My parents are very wealthy and well respected."

Angel said, "What is wrong with you? Why are you ill?"

Mary replied, "A few times, I felt dizzy at school and at home but didn't tell anyone as I didn't want to worry my parents. I thought it was nothing until one day when I was at school playing with my friends and I fainted.

"They told me 'My child, you rest while the doctors do your tests and you may have to stop over until we get the results.' At the time I was not so worried, Angel as I had my parents with me and that evening my friends and their parents came to see me.

"Later that evening, I saw my parents talking to the doctors outside the ward and saw how worried my parents were. When my parents finished talking to the doctors and came towards me, I was afraid.

"I thought the worst until my father said, 'Mary, you worry about nothing. We are taking you home in the morning and are going home while you sleep. See you in the morning.'"

After that, my parents gave me a big hug.

I knew then that something was wrong with me because I felt the pain sharp in my heart and knew my parents were hiding something from me. I prayed that night, 'Please Lord, make me better. If I have any kind of illness, please make me better.'

Then the next morning when I went home with my parents, I was told by them that I had blood cancer. I have leukaemia and my parents explained what it means and my mother was crying while my father was talking and also told me of all changes that will take place and what leukaemia does to a person. I asked my father if I was dying. At first my father didn't respond but when I asked again, my father said, 'No, Mary, I will not let anything happen to you. I will get the best doctors who will do your treatment.'

"As time passed, I went to hospital a few times, been checked by different doctors, had treatments but I'm not sure if the treatments are working. I knew I was going to die from the moment I started to lose my hair. I always see my parents stressed and sad, fighting with each other because of me. I know deep down my parents have done their best, but now it's in God's hands, so now you know, Angel why I was standing by the window, looking at the stars and asking God to answer my prayers and allow me to get better. I said my prayers and went towards my bed and that's when you entered my room with Companion."

Angel then said, "I'd like to ask you a few questions, but please tell me the truth."

Mary said, "I have no reason to lie, so ask me anything you want."

Angel's first question was, "When did you first ever pray to God, before or after you got ill?" and Mary replied, "I'd never prayed to God before. It's only since I got ill."

Angel's second question was, "Did you ever share or give any of your toys or dresses to your friends or children in need or who are poor and don't have anything?"

Mary replied with sadness on her face and said, "Dear Angel, I've never given anything I have to anyone. I keep everything for myself as they are gifts from my loved ones, I allow my friends to play with my toys but I've never given anything of mine."

Angel's third question to Mary was, "You have a cross by your bed. Did you and your parent's go to Church to pray every week or even once in a while?"

Mary's reply was, "My parents never go to Church to pray but a few times I have seen my parents praying in their bedroom when I walked in."

Angel asked her another question. "Mary, have you ever been bad to anyone – your parents or your friends at school – and do your friends come to visit you since you have been sick and off school?"

Mary, feeling flustered, asked, "Why are you asking me so many questions?"

Angel replied, "Please answer the final question and then I will tell you before I leave."

Mary said, trembling, "None of my friends have come to visit me since I have been ill, besides this one boy whose name is Abrielle who is blind and poor and his father works for my father in his business. Abrielle is smart, intelligent and a kind boy but no one at school likes him because he is blind and poor. I was surprised he came to visit me and brought me some fruit, but I told my mother to send him away from the front door and not to allow him to come to my bedroom as he was not my friend."

Angel replied back, with sadness in her eyes, "Mary, how could you do that and turn away that sweet blind boy named Abrielle who can't see but still came to visit you. You turned the little boy away; that is so cruel. Mary, if you wish to get better, I can help you, but you can't tell anyone you have a friend called Angel. This must be our secret and you must become a better person and do as I say. If not, then I will never return."

Mary said, "I promise I'll never tell anyone about you and I will change not because I want to get better but because I want to be a good person. As I was telling you everything Angel, I noticed inside me that I have been bad and selfish."

Angel replied, "OK, Mary, tomorrow is a new day, a new start of your life. You get up in the morning and thank God that he gave you another day to live and thank him for everything he has given you and your family. Always say the Lord's name when you eat. You should also thank the Lord for giving you a home, a family and for the lovely things you have, and every Sunday go to church and light a candle for your health, for your family and for everyone who has lost faith in God. Try to learn to give and share your things with people in need who don't have anything and the most important thing I'd like you to do is to go to Abrielle's house tomorrow, take some fruits and sweets for him and say you're very sorry for not allowing him to visit because, Mary, he is your true friend who came to visit you when none of your other friends came.

"Just because he is poor and blind does not mean you should be nasty to him. It's not his fault that he is poor and blind. How would you feel if you were poor and blind and had no friends?"

Mary replied, "It would hurt me, Angel if that happened to me, and I am very sorry, Angel. I understand I am wrong, but I can't go to visit him. Look at me, I am weak and have lost so much of my hair and look so ugly if anyone see me, they will laugh at me."

Angel replied back, "Don't worry what people do and say. Take no notice of them; this is a test for you to see what people are really like and learn from it. Your faith will make you strong and you will able to handle anything that takes place in your life and make you wiser. So, make your first step and go to Abrielle's house, no matter what anyone says, and always remember, Mary: real beauty comes from the inside not from the outside and it does not matter how you look from the outside. What matters is how you are from the inside."

Mary looked at Angel and Companion and said, "I promise you I will be his friend and I will always be there for him. I will also change for a better person and help people in need."

Angel said, "I am proud of you, Mary. I must leave now but I will be watching you and will come back when I see the changes in you."

Then Angel and Companion decided to leave. On their way home, they decided to go to visit Abrielle, and Abrielle was waiting for them and had fruits for them.

Angel said to Abrielle, "Didn't you go to sleep? It's so late, past your bed time."

Abrielle replied, "No, I was waiting for you because you promised that you would come and visit me."

Angel replied, "I was testing you."

Abrielle laughed and said, "Please have some fruit, I picked them from my back garden."

Angel was very happy, had some fruit and asked Abrielle, "If you could see again, what's the first thing you would like to see?"

Abrielle replied, "If I could, I would love to see God who created us all and thank him for everything. Because it's not possible for me to see, I would say if that if I could see again, then I would like to see my parents – my father, whose name is Robert and my mother whose name is Maya – and thank them for everything they have done for me, the love and support they given and for everything they taught me; my parents mean the world to me.

"I can still see the beautiful world through my parents' eyes and I'm blessed to have loving, caring parents. We might be poor, but we have so much love to give each other and are able to help people in need. It would be a pleasure to see the church I go to, every Sunday. I light a candle but not for myself, I light a candle for people in need who are worse off than me, for people who can't find work and can't provide for their families, and also for my friend Mary who attends my school and has blood cancer. She may not class me as her friend but I do class Mary as my friend. All I can do is pray for her so she gets well soon.

"If I could see again, then I would help Mary and many more people but what's important is to keep your faith and be strong. And good things do happen for people who wait."

Angel had tears in her eyes while she was listening to Abrielle and was so pleased with him and with the wise words he said, and Angel replied back to Abrielle, "You're a very special boy and your life will change very soon for the best, my friend and I will visit you again soon."

Angel and Companion flew through the window without realising that Abrielle's father Robert had seen them coming out of his son's bedroom window.

Robert had just come back from work doing the late shift. As his boss's daughter, Mary has cancer, her father did not spend much time at work.

When Robert opened the front door, his wife Maya was waiting for her husband and saw Robert looking speechless.

When Maya questioned Robert, "What is wrong?" Robert replied, "I just saw an angel and a white bird flying out of our son's bedroom window."

The parents ran upstairs to check on their son Abrielle and found him fast asleep in his bed but found his bedroom window open and fruit on the chair which Maya found very strange.

Robert closed Abrielle's bedroom window and they both went downstairs.

Maya said to Robert, "When I went to check on him, the window was closed." Robert replied, "Let's pray to God and thank him for everything and that it was an Angel that I saw. We should also thank the Lord that we are blessed and so is our child. We should not tell anyone and keep this secret, yes Robert no one will know. It's best, Robert, you have a wash while I warm your food."

Chapter Three

Meanwhile, Angel and Companion got home safely and Angel said to Companion, "For the next few nights I cannot go out because my brother John will be coming to my bedroom to play with me so I want you, Companion to go out in the day time and see how Mary is.

"Abrielle and I also want you to go to Abrielle's house, like a poor person asking for food and see the response you get."

Companion nodded his head and said yes. Angel and Companion went to the secret room and Angel got changed and went back to her bedroom.

She told Companion, "You sleep in the secret room because I don't want anyone to see you. If anyone comes to my bedroom, you should stay in the secret room, while I sleep in my bed."

Next morning, Angel told Companion when she went to the secret room to go to Mary's house and see if Mary had gone to visit Abrielle, and also check on Abrielle to see how he was doing.

"I will be spending the day at home doing some painting and spending time with John when he comes back from school. My brother did say he will come later on, so it's important I stay at home while you go and check on Abrielle and Mary."

So Companion left just before her brother came to her bedroom with breakfast. John told his sister, "Angel, I will come later on and visit you when the family goes to the neighbour's house for a birthday party."

Angel replied, "You must go as well John before our parents tell you off."

John replied, "I'd rather stay at home and spend my time with you."

Angel was so happy to see the love and affection her brother had towards her and after her brother John left, Angel had her breakfast and started to do her painting, thinking about Companion hoping he was OK.

Angel prayed to God, "Please protect Companion and give me the strength and willpower to help people in need, and for those who have lost their faith."

As Angel was saying her prayers, her mother knocked on the door to take the breakfast dishes and also she said to Angel, "Later on in the evening, the family and I will be going out to our neighbours' birthday party so make sure you behave and don't leave your bedroom to come downstairs. You're only allowed to use upstairs where the bedroom is."

Angel replied, "Mother, I will not come downstairs, and I will remain in my room unless I need to use the bathroom."

Her mother said, "That's OK. And I will bring your supper when I arrive back from our neighbours' house."

She then closed the bedroom door and went downstairs saying to herself that from then onwards, she was going to start giving Angel less food, and that way Angel would starve and die a lot sooner without anyone finding out.

Angel's mother, Anna had bad thoughts crossing her mind and started to believe that Angel was a sinner for the reason she had an unknown form of disease and her face was disfigured. She thought Angel was a bad omen for this family, so the mother had cruel plans to kill Angel slowly.

She didn't know that Angel was pure in heart with no disease and looked prettier now then she had done before. Since the accident, Angel's mother Anna had always made Angel cover her face. She had no idea that her daughter had been cured by a miracle which was a gift from God, who had answered Angel's prayers.

How little did Angel's mother know! Angel was not a sinner; instead Angel was a chosen child who had powers and that is what Companion was saying to himself while he heard Angel's mother talking to herself in the kitchen, because Companion was behind the table as he was looking for food.

Then he flew out the kitchen window and went straight into Angel's bedroom. Angel was happy to see Companion and hold him, and she said, "I could be wrong but I believe my mother has cruel plans in store for me. I feel afraid and restless, Companion."

When her family arrived home, Angel's father asked Anna, "Did you give Angel supper?"

For the first time, Anna lied to her husband, "Yes, I gave Angel supper."

Companion flew through the window and went into the small kitchen window which was always open and found some bread for Angel.

When Companion went back to Angel's bedroom with the bread, Angel questioned Companion. "Where did you get the bread from?"

Companion wrote on the wall, with his feathers, from downstairs kitchen.

Angel thanked Companion for the bread and also smiled at him and said, "I did not know you could write with your feathers."

Then Companion also wrote names on the wall who they needed to see tonight and the names were Abrielle and Mary.

Angel, in a joyful mood, said, "Yes, we will leave soon after I've eaten." Angel was saying to Companion whilst she was eating, "I hope Mary has visited Abrielle." She then asked, "So, Companion, did you see Mary going to Abrielle's house as I asked you to do?"

Companion nodded his head and said, "Yes."

Angel was so happy and said, "I can't wait to see Abrielle, so I can ask him how it went with Mary."

As soon as Angel finished eating, she went to her secret room to get ready, put her dress on and her necklace, which has powers and said to Companion, "Let's fly through the window and go to visit Abrielle."

So they went to see Abrielle and noticed his bedroom window was closed and he was sitting on his bed looking very sad. Angel knocked on his window and Abrielle went running towards them with a smile, as he knew it was Angel and Companion.

As he opened the window, Angel and Companion came inside, and Abrielle said, "The window was closed because my parents put me in bed."

Angel replied, "You have no reason to say sorry; instead you're very lucky to have loving parents who care about you."

Angel asked Abrielle, "How did you know it was us knocking on your window?"

Abrielle smiled and replied, "Angel, I may be blind and can't see, but yet I can sense and feel. I just knew it was you."

Angel replied, "Now you know why I said to you before that you're a special boy."

Abrielle smiled and said, "OK. But I have so much to tell you! You'll never believe who came to visit me today."

Angel paused and replied, "Before you tell me, how was your day and why were you sitting on your bed looking so sad?"

"I didn't know when you would be back. That's the reason why I could not sleep and was sitting on the bed, looking sad."

Angel replied, "Abrielle, in future please do not sit up and wait for me. Sorry I came late tonight. In future I will try and come early and if I come late then I will wake you up."

Abrielle replied, "I am sorry. It will not happen again and I will not be awake until late."

Abrielle then offered fruit and sweets to Angel and Angel asked, "Where did you get all these sweets from?"

Abrielle said, "Please have some, then I will tell you about the day I had and who came to visit me."

Angel replied, "Thank you for the fruit and sweets."

While Angel was sitting on the bed with Companion and eating, Abrielle told Angel it was Mary who had been to visit him that day and brought all those sweets, fruit, colouring books and pencils.

"I was shocked when my father told me Mary had come to visit me. I saw her standing on my doorstep and she apologised for being rude when I went down to visit her – 'Abrielle, I am very sorry for the fact I sent you away, when you came to visit me. I soon realised I was really bad to you knowing you were the only one who came to visit me; none of my friends came to visit me since I became ill. I've realised you're my true friend who cares about me and I used to be so nasty to when I was at school.' Mary cried and said, 'I am sorry for everything. Will you please forgive me Abrielle?'

"And I replied back, 'Please Mary, don't cry. I forgive you for everything,' and Mary replied back, 'How did you know I was crying while I was talking when you can't see and you're blind?' I replied that I could tell from the tone of her voice that she was crying.

"Mary then said happily, 'You're so good and I am such a bad person, that's why I'm so ill, and I said, 'Please do not blame yourself for your illness. Have faith in God and you will get better and I also will pray for you and my parents will pray for you.'

"Mary replied, 'Thank you so much Abrielle, oh silly me I forgot to give you the stuff I brought for you. Look Abrielle, I brought you fruit, sweets, colouring books and pencils' and I said there was no need for all that.

"I told her, 'Mary, just to see you here is a pleasure,' and Mary replied, 'I wanted to bring all this because Abrielle is my special friend who is so caring and forgiving.

"I said, 'Thank you Mary,' and my father Robert then said, 'Abrielle, why don't you take your friend Mary to your bedroom and while you kids talk and play, I will bring you some drinks and biscuits.

"So Mary came with me to my bedroom and said I had a nice bedroom. She asked if I'd drawn all the pictures that are on the wall and I said yes.

"I asked Mary to sit down and have some of these lovely sweets she'd brought me but Mary replied, 'Oh no, Abrielle, I brought them for you.' I told her I believe in sharing, so please have some.

"So Mary helped herself to the sweets while she was looking at the pictures that I had drawn and painted. As she was looking around my room, Mary then said, 'Abrielle, I am well impressed with your pictures. They are fantastic. You could make a living by drawing and painting pictures. I just laughed and asked which one she thought was the best.

"Mary said the Church one, where everyone was praying and had a cross but she couldn't understand how I could draw and paint so well when I was blind.

"I told her I had a talent which meant I can see things in my mind, and then draw and paint them. I can also smell things and can tell from people's voices. I might be blind but my mind and imagination senses things and can tell who people are and if they are happy or sad.

"Mary said that was so amazing and I said the reason I'd asked her what pictures she liked the most was because they're not pictures or paintings, they're my dreams. For example there's a picture where you can see kids in the school playground, playing with the ball, but what she didn't notice was the one lonely boy sitting on the bench.

That represents me, wishing how nice it would be if I was also playing with other kids. Also, the painting she liked the most – the church painting – is also my favourite picture and my dream that one day I pray I have my eye sight back so I can see everyone and the priest, because the Church is the main part of my life. My parents have been taking me to Church since I was a baby. The Church gives me peace when I am sad. The Lord puts a smile on my face, it gives me strength and hope that's why I painted a picture of the Church. I asked Mary why she thought I drew the picture of a doctor and a patient. Mary then said, 'Abrielle, you dream about a doctor doing a treatment for you to get your eyesight back.' I told her she was wrong, that it's a picture of me treating a patient; that what I'd like to be when I grow up is a doctor and treat people. I told Mary, all these pictures had a meaning to my dreams. If they come true or not, I will leave it in God's hands, as he knows what's best for me, but I can never make a living in drawing pictures and paintings because it's my hobby, and dreams are not for sale. I told Mary that she liked the church painting, she could have it and put it in her bedroom.

"Mary replied, 'Abrielle I cannot have this painting it's yours and it means so much to you,' but I replied, 'Mary, it's a gift for you from me and I will make another painting like this for myself. You're my special friend, Mary, and it will give me pleasure if you'd please accept this painting as a gift.' Mary replied, 'You're so amazing, Abrielle, of course I will accept this gift. I am so happy I came to visit you Abrielle, spending time with you I've learnt so much from you Abrielle. I will pray for you that you get your eyesight back and all your dreams come true for you, Abrielle. You have a good heart with good thoughts, unlike me being so selfish and always thinking about myself, never sharing my stuff with anybody. Even when I got ill, I thought I'd get better since my parents are so wealthy, as I'd have the best treatment that money could buy and I'd be cured and never had faith in God. I always thought that money could buy anything I wanted. Oh my God, I was so wrong. No wonder I am ill and dying.'

"I told Mary not to blame herself as it was a test from God. 'Who said you will not get better? Do not blame what the doctors say! You must learn to have faith in God. Only God can do miracles, not doctors,' and I also told her to go to Church and pray every Sunday. I told her she'd find peace and hope, and learn to share and give. It's true that I may be poor and so is my family as my father only earns enough to provide for the family, but yet we are very happy for what we have and our main wealth is our faith in God.

"I told her that she has everything in life and even if I never get my eyesight back, and remain blind for the rest of my life, I will not be sad. I will still be happy like I am now and neither would I lose my faith. Mary looked at me and said, 'You're so right. You've made me look at life from a different angle, Abrielle and of course I will change for the best, not because I want God to cure me but because I want to be a better person from now on. Will you help and guide me?' I told her of course I would and that I would always help and be there for her.

"At that moment, my mother Maya knocked on the door with drinks and biscuits for us and said, 'Sorry for the delay, I was preparing for supper,' and she asked Mary if she would like to stay for supper. Mary replied that it would be an honour to stay for supper and after the family had their supper, I walked Mary home and she said to me, 'I had a lovely day and you're always welcome to visit me at my home.' I then said, 'Thanks, Mary, we will meet again tomorrow.' Mary said, 'Of course, Abrielle, I will be waiting for you in the morning and I replied, 'I will be at your home after breakfast time.'

"Mary cheerfully said OK and thanked me for walking her home and said she hoped I got home safely. I thanked her, went home and told my parents what a lovely day I'd had with Mary, what we'd done and what we'd spoken about.

"My parents said they were glad that I had a good friend and was there for her, knowing she was very ill, and that by offering support and guiding her, I'd made them so proud for giving Mary my favourite painting of the church as well.

"I told them I will do my best to help Mary to find her faith and support her as she was so lost at this present time. I asked if I could visit Mary in the morning as she'd invited me to go to spend the day at her house. My parents said, 'Of course, my child you can go and visit your friend Mary.'"

Angel and Companion were so happy after Abrielle told them the day he had with Mary and what they had done.

Angel said, "I am so proud of you, Abrielle and now you got a friend to play with."

Abrielle replied back, "Of course, I know this is the best day I've had in a long time."

Angel replied, "We must leave now but I will see you soon. Until then, you take care of yourself and your family and Mary."

Abrielle replied, "Since I met you Angel, everything is going well for me. I could never thank you enough."

Angel replied, "I didn't do anything, Abrielle, it's the Lord who answered your prayers. Always remember, never lose your faith no matter how difficult it maybe."

Abrielle replied, "I will never forget and it's pleasure to have you and Companion in my life."

Angel replied, "You must sleep now, Abrielle because it's past your bed time and we will see you soon. Sweet dreams!"

After Angel and Companion left, Abrielle closed his bedroom window, said his prayers and went to sleep.

Chapter Four

As the days went by Abrielle and Mary become good friends, spending more time with each other after school. At weekends, Mary gave her clothes and toys to the poor kids as she had a bedroom full of clothes and toys. She also shared her stuff with other kids, and she started to go to Church with Abrielle and his family.

Mary's parents soon saw the difference in Mary's attitude and they were so proud of their daughter, that she was no longer sad and depressed, and happy that she no longer stayed in her bedroom all day along, and had a true friend in Abrielle who was always there for her and supported Mary in every way possible.

Mary changed from a spoilt and selfish girl into a sweet, loving, caring girl.

Mary's parents and neighbours were surprised to see the changes in Mary whilst, on the other hand, Angel's parents were still the same towards her. Nothing had changed for poor Angel.

As soon as Angel arrived home, she said to Companion, "I hope my family can change as well and love me the way I am, for better or for worse and be proud to introduce me to the neighbours, saying that's my daughter, Angel, and be the family they used to be before I got sick, of course.

"Companion, I can go now and tell my family that I am better and I never had any disease in the first place and the Lord has made me better because I never lost my faith. I've also got a friend called Companion and God chose me to help people in need, and who are ill and gave me special powers. Then, of course, my family will accept me and I will forgive my family for all the pain they gave me.

"The only thing that's stopping me from telling my family is that I don't know whether they will accept me because I am better and no longer ill, and the fact I have been chosen by God to help people in need. Or would my family accept me because my parents are deeply sorry for the way they treated me when I fell ill, and they have regrets for everything they have done to me?

"From the moment I fell ill, my mother has been starving me. So it's best that I don't tell my family anything because I want my family to accept me for the way I am in their eyes. I'm a sick child and my parents haven't accepted their mistakes for the way they treated me and kept me locked away in this room away from the outside world."

For these reasons Angel told Companion, "My family will not know the truth about me and if it was not for you Companion, God knows what would have happened to me. I am so grateful that I that I have you, the Lord, and my faith."

Angel and Companion hugged each other and fell asleep on the bed.

Angel was woken the next morning by her brother knocking on the door to give her breakfast and Angel was surprised how she had gone to sleep without getting changed and not hiding Companion in the secret cupboard.

Angel told her brother, "John, please leave the breakfast outside the room as I am not ready."

John left Angel's breakfast outside the room and said, "I will come and see you after school."

Angel replied, "OK", then got changed and hid Companion in the secret room. She then opened her bedroom door, got her breakfast and after locking her bedroom door, got Companion out of the secret room so they could both have breakfast together and spend the day in the bedroom.

Angel was painting a picture of herself dressed in an Angel outfit with Companion on her arm. At that moment Angel heard the footsteps of someone coming upstairs and it was her mother Anna knocking on the door.

Angel hid Companion and also her painting under the bed. She answered the door and her mother gave Angel some muffin cakes for lunch and told her, "Make sure you eat it as it's good for your health, I've put some protein in these cakes for you."

Angel thanked her mother and closed the door. Her mother got suspicious, wondering why Angel had locked the door. Her mother went back and knocked on the door again and insisted that Angel open the door at once.

As Angel opened the door, she said to her mother, "What is wrong?"

Her mother replied, "What are you hiding from me?"

Angel replied, "Nothing, mother, why did you ask?"

Her mother replied, "Why were you in a rush to lock the door?"

Angel replied, "Because you can't bear seeing me and you wish I was dead. I can see it in your eyes, mother. Answer me, am I right or wrong?"

Her mother refused to answer Angel and looked away from her as she was feeling guilty. Anna looked around the room then left.

Angel felt so angry and she locked her bedroom door, put the muffins on the table, and got Companion and her painting from underneath the bed.

As Companion went towards the muffins, Angel stopped him and said, "No, do not eat them as it feels strange that my mother brought them to my bedroom and insisted that I eat them. I felt that my mother looked guilty when she gave them to me."

So Companion didn't touch the cakes as Angel continued with her painting. Companion saw a little mouse that went towards the muffins and it ate some of the muffin. Companion started to fly around Angel and disturbed her from painting.

Angel knew something was wrong so she looked behind her and saw Companion sitting near the muffins. At this point Angel noticed the mouse was dead and looked so shocked and said to Companion, "Where did this mouse come from?"

"Oh Lord, the dear mouse ate the muffin and died which means my mother lied. It didn't have protein in the cakes; it was poison. I knew something was wrong. My own mother wanted me to die. I will not eat from this home again."

She said to Companion, "Thank God, I stopped you from eating these muffins. Imagine if you ate them, I would have lost you, Companion. I know it was a sign from God to let me know what my mother's intentions were and that's why this mouse came and ate these muffins to warn me."

Angel cried and said, "I can't believe my mother, who gave me birth, tried to kill me," and after that Angel wiped her tears and said to Companion, "When the time is right, we will leave here and go where it's safe as I feel my life is in danger.

"Until then we must focus on Abrielle and Mary and other people in need."

At that point Angel heard a knock on her door, and it was her brother John. Angel told Companion, "Please take the little mouse and bury him while I answer the door to my brother."

So Companion left and took the mouse with him and Angel threw the muffins in the bins and then answered the door.

John asked quickly why it had taken so long to open the door and Angel replied, "Because I needed to cover my face before I opened the door. I don't want you to be afraid when you see me."

John replied, "I don't care what you look like, as you're my big sister and I love you very much indeed. I've brought you supper."

Angel took the supper, put it on the table and told John, "Please sit on the chair as I need to speak to you. I know you care a great deal for me but the only time you come to my bedroom is when you bring me food, those are the only times."

John said sadly, "Am I not allowed to come after the family are asleep? I could play games with you."

Angel replied, "No, because when the family finds out, you come and play with me and get sweets for me, they will be very angry with you. I do not want you to get in trouble because of me. I am very sorry, but it's for the best and I'm not alone, I have got the Lord with me. I've also got my paintings to keep me busy."

John replied sadly, "OK, Angel. If you need anything, you just ask me."

Angel replied, "OK, John I will let you know and also I am very grateful I have a loving brother like you, who has always been there for me. How is our brother James? He never comes to bring me food. It's always you."

John replied, "That is because as far as James is concerned, he no longer has a sister, because our mother has taught him to forget you, and that you don't have long to live."

Angel sadly replied, "What about our father?"

John replied, "He never talks about you any more, it's as if you don't exist and, anyway, he keeps himself busy with work. But I will never forget you Angel, because you're my sweet loving sister."

Angel hugged John and said, "Thank you for being caring and honest with me."

As John was about to leave, he said to Angel, "Mother said, 'Did you like the muffins and did you eat them all?'"

Angel said, "Yes, they were nice and you can take the plate and tell Mother thank you for the supper as well."

John replied, "OK, Angel. Oh, by the way, I forgot to tell you Christmas is coming up soon."

Angel said, "How long is left until Christmas Day?"

John said, "Only two weeks left, and what would you like to have for Christmas, Angel?"

Angel replied, "I have everything I need, but I wish my family and everyone a good Christmas and to be in good health."

John replied, "Well, I will get you a nice gift for Christmas."

Angel replied, "No, brother, all I want is for my family to be happy, and that will be the best gift I can get along with having a good brother like you. You must now leave, brother, you'll get questioned as to why it took you so long."

John gave Angel a hug and left. Angel decided not to eat the supper as she knew it was poisoned. Companion soon arrived and Angel asked whether he had buried the mouse.

Companion nodded his head and said, "Yes."

Angel then said to him, "That's good, but it's sad this poor mouse had to die because of my mother. My brother brought me supper not knowing whether it was poisoned, I refused to eat it."

So Companion brought Angel bread from the kitchen without anyone knowing.

Angel thanked Companion and said, "Christmas will be coming up soon so I will draw paintings on the walls of Angels and Jesus and Mary in our room and we will have our own Christmas."

Companion was happy and was flying with joy.

Chapter Five

As the days went by, Angel said to Companion, "It's time we went to visit Abrielle and Mary, as it's Christmas Eve today."

Companion and Angel were on their way to see Abrielle and a little girl who was standing by her bedroom window saw the Angel flying and went running to her parents to tell them.

As her parents found it hard to believe, they said, "You had a dream, Rina, there are no Angels." So Rina went back to her bedroom; she knew what she'd seen and sat by her window all night, hoping she may see the Angel through her window.

When Angel arrived at Abrielle's bedroom window, she noticed the bedroom window was already open, so Angel and Companion went inside Abrielle's room and noticed that Abrielle was sitting on his bed, very worried.

Angel asked what was wrong and Abrielle replied, "I am so happy to see you, Angel but why haven't you been to visit me?"

Angel replied, "Because I was busy and also I wanted you to spend more time with Mary. Something is still bothering you, Abrielle, why are you so worried?"

Abrielle replied, "My friend Mary is very ill and I heard my parents talking to each other that tonight may be Mary's last night. She is dying and I am going to lose my friend. I spent the whole day at Mary's house and I prayed for her to get better. And Mary said to me that she not afraid of dying, but at least got to do some good deeds before the Lord takes her.

"She said she was sad because her parents were going to miss her so much and because she didn't get enough time to spend with me. She said she was happy that I had entered into her life and changed her into a better person. She said I would always be her special friend, and she would always be watching over me.

"And she said she'd say to the Lord to give me eyes to see everything and for me to always do well in life.

"Mary asked if she could ask me one last thing and that was to please always be there for her parents. I promised her that I would always be there for her parents and also stated, 'I don't care what the doctor says, as I only believe in God, and I knew you will not die. Please don't lose your faith Mary and stay awake until I come back. I must go home but I will arrive back very soon.'

"That's what I said to Mary, so please, Angel help me to get Mary better. She is a changed person, and she is a very loving and caring person who donates most of her things to the poor kids, not because she is dying but for the fact she's realised she was a very selfish and uncaring person before.

"Her illness has changed her into a better person. I do understand that we all must go to God one day, but I want Mary to live her life. If there is anything I want for Christmas Day, tomorrow, then I pray that the Lord allows Mary to live a long life."

Angel was very happy about Abrielle's brief true, friendship towards Mary and said to him, "You ask for nothing for yourself from the Lord but you ask for your friend Mary. You've very special, Abrielle. You don't need to worry about Mary because I am going to visit her now and you just pray to the Lord that Mary gets well soon."

Abrielle replied, "Of course I will pray for Mary, but please, Angel, be careful when you go as there are so many people at Mary's house tonight because it's Christmas Eve and they're there to visit Mary."

Angel replied, "Thank you for letting me know. I will be careful."

Abrielle noticed that Angel didn't sound good and asked Angel if she was OK, to which Angel replied, "I am OK, but can I please have some water?"

"Of course," said Abrielle. "I'll bring you some water and fruit."

Angel was thankful for Abrielle's kindness and promised him she'd be back before midnight.

Both she and Companion made their way to Mary's home. As they got nearer to Mary's bedroom window, they noticed the priest and the doctor leaving her bedroom.

Mary was lying on her bed as Angel and Companion came through the window and Mary was very pleased to see them. Mary was sad and asked Angel to lock her bedroom door before anyone came inside to discover them.

Angel locked the door, sat next to Mary and noticed she was so ill, she could hardly speak, and the only thing Mary said was, "I am not afraid to die, but am sad as I am leaving my loving parents behind and my friend Abrielle and you Angel."

As the tears welled up in Mary's eyes, Angel smiled at Mary, wiped her tears and said, "You're not going to die, it's true. You were ill for a short time; it was a test from God, Mary, to see if you have faith in God or not, and to see if you learnt from the mistakes you made, and it's changed you for a better person.

"You have realised that wealth is not everything and if you have wealth you should share, which you did, by helping people in need. You've learnt to share, you've learnt to love others and you've also learnt beauty is from the inside not from outside, as the beauty from the outside fades with time, or can get damaged anytime in life. But the real beauty is from inside and will never fade away as it will glow from the outside.

"Mary, you will live your life and always be happy and grateful for what you have and always help people in need. You have a true friend in Abrielle, who will always be there for you.

"Now I will show you something, but first you must close your eyes."

So Mary closed her eyes. Angel took her necklace off and laid the necklace on Mary's chest and the light went right through Mary's body and she noticed the changes in Mary's health.

Angel then took her necklace back and put it around her neck and asked Mary to get up. As soon as Mary opened her eyes, she noticed she could move her hands and was able to speak.

Mary looked at Angel and said, "You're a true angel, and you've given me my life back."

Mary hugged Angel and thanked her. There was someone knocking on Mary's door and Angel said, "I must leave now as I promised to see Abrielle, your friend before midnight."

Mary asked, "Will I see you again?"

Angel replied, "I will always watch over you and Mary, never lose your faith."

As Angel and Companion were about to go through the window, Mary's father, her doctor and the priest broke the door and came in to see whether Mary was OK and ask why she had locked the door.

They saw Angel and Companion fly through the window and were shocked as they also realised that Mary was cured from her illness.

The priest said it was a miracle that the Lord had done for Mary; everyone was so happy and thanking the Lord.

The doctor said, "Before I came here, my daughter Rina did say she saw an angel flying past her bedroom window, but I didn't believe her. Angels and miracles do exist!"

Mary replied, "I never lose faith, no matter what happens in life and Angel has gone to see my friend Abrielle."

At this point everyone left in a rush to see Angel at Abrielle's house, and all the neighbours were happy to see Mary cured.

They got to Abrielle's house and his family were shocked and surprised to see Mary had recovered. Abrielle was so happy and they wondered what all these people were doing here including the neighbours.

Everyone was asking Abrielle whether the Angel had come to visit him.

Abrielle was speechless, and Mary said it was Angel who had cured her and given her a second chance and told her that she was going to visit.

Abrielle's parents questioned him about what Mary was talking about, and Abrielle replied, "If I told you, Dad and Mum, you would have never believed me, and I promised Angel I'd never tell anyone. It was a secret."

"Angel has not come to visit me yet as everyone is waiting and hoping to see Angel and praying to see the glimpse of Angel."

One of the neighbours phoned the local news reporter and told the reporter about Angel and the miracle.

As the reporters were on their way, Angel came back as she promised Abrielle just before midnight. Everyone was standing in the road and in Abrielle's house with candles in their hands so they could see a glimpse of Angel and Companion.

Angel and Companion were flying around Abrielle and in such a strong light which left everyone shocked and speechless.

Angel told Abrielle, "Open your eyes!" and then Abrielle saw the Angel and Companion fly away and everyone got the chance to see the glimpse of Angel and Companion including the reporters who just arrived in time.

Abrielle was looking at his parents and said, "I can see! I've got my eyesight back! Look at this pendant which Angel put around my neck! I will never take it off."

Abrielle, his parents, Mary and everyone else was so happy for the miracles and praising the Lord. Snow began to fall and everyone realised it was Christmas Day

Everyone was wishing each other 'Happy Christmas', hugging each other and praising the Lord for everything and miracles.

And that angels do exist.